D0493628

Written by

Edmund Squibb

Illustrations by

Margaret Doig

Published by The Vulcan To The Sky Club

Vulcan is a trademark of BAE Systems plc.
Vulcan To The Sky, the Vulcan planform and XH558 are trademarks of the Vulcan To The Sky Trust, used with permission.
Vulcan Ventures is a trademark of E. Squibb and M. Doig

Prepared for print by www.underthefloor.co.uk
Digital image scanning by www.cadmeleon.co.uk Alloa, Scotland
Printed in the UK by Stephens & George Print Group

ISBN 978-0-9563146-2-8

For Sophie

There was a typical autumn chill in the air, and the hangar was absolutely freezing. FiveFiveEight didn't mind, she was used to the cold. As she opened her tired eyes, she could see teeny-weeny droplets of water dripping off her nose. She couldn't look for long, because it made her cross-eyed, and she really didn't want to stay that way forever! As she peered around the darkened hangar, nothing *seemed* different to any other day, but FiveFiveEight just had a funny feeling in her wings – that feeling we all have when we know *something* is different but just can't say *what*.

FiveFiveEight sat and pondered for a while. The last few months had been strange – *very* strange! Taken away from all her friends outside, she'd been shoved into a dull and boring hangar. She was certainly now nice and dry, but she'd easily swap it for not being so lonely. She desperately missed her friends; Comet, Hunter, Buccaneer, Jet Provost (who liked to be called simply "JP") – she even missed Guppy's very VERY loud snoring! But most of all she missed Victor, the only other V-Bomber on the airfield; they used to swap stories of amazing missions, secret destinations and scary landings! Although they had always competed with one another in the Royal Air Force – who was the fastest, who flew higher, who carried the heaviest load – now retired, they were firm friends. Friends Forever! It seemed an eternity that FiveFiveEight had been locked away facing that plain and featureless hangar wall, and exactly *why* she had been was still a complete mystery.

During that time, though, some very odd things had been happening; she'd seen hundreds of strangers come and go, some dressed in dapper suits, others in greasy overalls. They'd all do the same thing – look FiveFiveEight up and down, stroke their chins and say, "Hmmmmmm", usually with heavy frowns on their faces. At night, the hangar lights would be switched off, and FiveFiveEight would immediately begin to nod off into a deep and heavy sleep. Her dreams were always the same, and had been since the day that she'd retired – Blue Skies and Fluffy White Clouds!

For many months, her old friend Crew Chief and his helpers had been removing all her bits and bobs, carefully examining them before tying big brown tags to them and placing them neatly in boxes. This wasn't a new experience for her, as she remembered the same thing happening many years ago in the RAF to make sure she was in tip-top condition to fly. But those days were long gone, and she was too old to fly any longer. All she had to rely on were her memories and dreams of soaring through the clouds into a beautiful blue sky.

This time, however, much more of FiveFiveEight was being dismantled than she'd ever experienced before! Her undercarriage had been removed, leaving her perched high on huge metal jacks and feeling very helpless. As the weeks went by, more and more of her had been removed, tagged, put into bags or boxes, and carted off to who-knows-where. Even her mighty Olympus engines had been taken out months ago and zipped into things that looked like giant sleeping bags. FiveFiveEight had only one thought in her mind, though, a horrible and scary thought! In fact, it was the most horrible thought that any once-proud aeroplane could ever have: FiveFiveEight had become convinced that she was being "RTS"! If you ever go near an aeroplane, never ever mention those three dreaded letters – they stand for "Reduced to Spares"! Being taken apart piece by piece might help other sick aeroplanes, but it's every aeroplane's worst nightmare – becoming nothing more than a few boxes of bits.

One thing, though, was very confusing. Just as quickly as her components were being carted away, gleaming new ones were being brought *back!* What on Earth was going on? This couldn't be "Reduced to Spares", surely? One day she even saw Crew Chief struggling with what appeared to be her wheels – bright glimmering silver, each with two glossy black tyres on.

She had known Crew Chief for ages – a kindly looking man with a huge smile and glasses perched on the end of his nose. He used to look after her when she was still an important Vulcan, defending her country, but after she'd retired long ago, she hadn't seen him for many years. Why he had returned was just *another* mystery. Even so, his spanners were just as cold and unwelcome as she remembered.

As the weeks and months passed, FiveFiveEight was meticulously put back together. She now had four brand new engines, completely new wiring, new undercarriage, new fuel tanks, new panels – new *everything* it seemed – even some fresh paint here and there. She had thankfully been lowered back onto the ground again, supporting herself on her own legs and wheels for the first time in a long *long* while. Crew Chief then magically produced some giant scales to see how much difference the months of feverish work had made (but it wouldn't be right to divulge a lady's weight, now would it?). FiveFiveEight had no means of knowing how she *looked*, but she knew she *felt* fantastic – like a Brand New Vulcan!

Then, very early one morning, as she felt another drip of moisture trickle down her nose, a shaft of daylight cut through the gloom of the hangar, waking FiveFiveEight with a start. Immediately, the sound of chatter filled the air as Crew Chief and his engineers paraded in through the open door. FiveFiveEight always tried to eavesdrop on the conversations, usually peppered with laughter, but she would normally only catch the odd word or two. But today there was another voice – a voice that she *instantly* recognised – a voice she hadn't heard for many, *many* years! *Surely, it couldn't be?*

IT WAS!!!!!!!!

A tall upright gentleman, wearing a crisp, white roll-neck shirt under his leather jacket, walked toward her with that same twinkle in his eye she remembered so well. His hair was a little greyer than she remembered it to be, but it was definitely the same man. The Pilot! Now she *knew* something was afoot – The Pilot had been her best friend in the entire World many years ago, and she hadn't seen *him* for even longer than Crew Chief! She'd never known his full name, but of all the people that she'd seen come and go in her long RAF career, The Pilot was the one she missed most of all. They had shared so many incredible journeys together (a couple of scary ones, too, which FiveFiveEight would rather forget!) and he was the only man who *truly* understood her. Her vast frame filled with glee when she felt a reassuring pat on her leg, as her friend walked around admiring the wonderful work that had been done to her. The Pilot was back, and that could mean only *one thing*!

As The Pilot and his Aircrew settled into their seats and examined all her gleaming new instruments, FiveFiveEight's mind wandered back to her days in the RAF – a time when Vulcans had the most important job in Britain: Guardians of our Skies, keeping people safe. After nearly thirty years, however, Vulcans had passed this proud duty on to much younger and fitter aeroplanes (and even some Submarines!). But even after all her Vulcan friends had retired, FiveFiveEight carried on alone for years afterward, flying around the country to countless different airshows where, despite her advancing years, she would astonish all the little faces looking up at her as she roared her one-hundred-ton frame around the sky – just as nimbly as an aeroplane half her size and half her age!

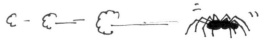

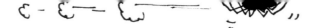

FiveFiveEight had always known that her fun couldn't last forever, though. She was getting more and more worn out, and some of her spare parts were becoming very difficult to find. Eventually, the RAF decided it was time for her to retire and found a quiet little airfield where she could go. There were even some of her old friends there, also retired, so she'd never feel lonely. For a few years, she and The Pilot were sometimes allowed to fire up her engines, taxy onto the runway, and deafen all the visitors as she thundered up the tarmac. FiveFiveEight loved to show off the enormous white tail 'chute that helped slow her down. Sadly, she was never allowed to take off – just as she was ready to leap into the air, The Pilot would say, "Now now, old girl, as much as I know you'd *love* to, it's Against The Rules!". Occasionally, if the wind was right, he would let her lift her nosewheel off the ground, and she would close her eyes and imagine she was flying again.

Then one day, once she'd shut her engines down, she watched as The Pilot slowly climbed out, looked up at her with a little smile, then turned and walked away for what she knew was the very last time. As the years had passed, sure enough, no more pretend take-offs, no more kicking up clouds of dust with her fabulous engines, no more little faces gawking at her as she roared past. It had really seemed like the end.

Until NOW!

At that moment, FiveFiveEight heard the hangar doors open even wider, with their usual "*squeak squeak* CLUNK! *squeak squeak* CLUNK!*", until they were fully open – something which she hadn't witnessed for months – NO, YEARS! From the corner of her eye, she noticed the scruffy old Tractor chugging into the hangar before coming to a halt directly beneath her nose, and in no time at all she felt the towbar being hooked onto her nosewheel. Before she knew it, the little Tractor was clenching his teeth and, with a very red face and much puffing, wheezing and grunting, was pushing FiveFiveEight out into the dazzling sunlight. It was a mystery how this tiny machine could move such a massive aeroplane. He'd often been asked, but he'd always answer in the same grumpy tone: "Gearing!" he'd mumble, before trundling off with a face like thunder,

"Gearing!". None of the aeroplanes ever had the guts to ask him to explain what "Gearing" was, but the general opinion was that it must be something special he'd had for breakfast!

It was *fantastic* to be out and about again and, as she felt the warmth of the sun on her back, FiveFiveEight glanced across and could clearly see all her old friends looking on – Victor, Comet, JP, and that odd little one who spoke with a strange accent. He was Polish, apparently, not that FiveFiveEight knew what that meant. Even the Trusty Old Fire Tender was there, standing in the usual puddle of water that always caused him huge embarrassment. The aeroplanes liked to make fun of his "Waterworks Problem", but deep down they all knew just how important he was at the airfield should things go wrong.

The Tractor, having caught his breath, turned around and began to move once more – forward this time. V-e-r-y slowly, he pulled FiveFiveEight away from the hangar, which seemed to get smaller and smaller to the extent that she began to wonder how she'd ever managed to fit inside in the first place! They continued on past all the parts of the airfield she hadn't seen for such a long time. Everything looked just as she remembered, just as she'd dreamt about whilst staring endlessly at that dreadful blank wall for all those years.

Soon they were at the end of the runway, and FiveFiveEight stared at the long, grey ribbon of tarmac that seemed to disappear into a tiny dot away in the distance, with its white centreline shimmering and glimmering in the heat-haze. The Aircrew started their long list of equipment checks, all carried out in the usual garbled manner over the intercom. Why The Pilot couldn't just say "GO!" had long been a cause of frustration to FiveFiveEight – *she* knew that all her systems were functioning, so why couldn't he just *trust* her? "Humans!", she thought to herself, rolling her eyes.

As FiveFiveEight began to spool up her four Olympus engines, she heard a faint voice. "Good luck FiveFiveEight!", it said in an eager tone. "Go for it!", said another from the same place. It was the Lightning Twins! When they weren't busy squabbling, the two fighter jets were inseparable, typically spending the entire time poking fun at anything and everything they could think of – usually each other! FiveFiveEight hadn't noticed that they were right behind her, tucked away in their shiny new hangar. *That* was new – it really *had* been a long time since FiveFiveEight had sat at the end of that runway, eagerly awaiting one of her thunderous takeoff runs. She was so *excited!*

"Three.....Two.....One.....GO!", said The Pilot, as he pushed FiveFiveEight's throttle levers forward and released her brakes. She immediately felt her nose rise as she surged forward. For a brief moment her heart sank as she felt herself veering to the left – one of her brakes was a little sticky – but The Pilot expertly guided her back onto the centreline. As the enormous thrust of her engines pushed her forward, with their characteristic howl and roar, she quickly gathered speed along the hot tarmac.

"Twenty..........Thirty......" – The Pilot called out her speed – WOW! She hadn't done this in *years!* She wanted it to last forever, knowing that all too soon, at eighty knots, The Pilot would pull the throttles back and apply her brakes. She could feel the wind rushing past her nose as she continued to roar along the runway, making her eyes water as it always had in the past. "Seventy.......Eighty........"

"This is it", she sighed, waiting for that familiar jolt as her 'chute deployed. "Ninety.........One Hundred........", The Pilot continued. No 'chute? No brakes? FiveFiveEight was *still* accelerating! More garbled numbers from The Pilot – in her confusion, *she'd* lost count! – "What's going on?", she pondered, as more and more runway zoomed under her vast delta wings. Only a second later, she had her answer...

"WOOHOOOOOOOOO!", she yelled at the top of her voice as she leapt off the ground. "I'm......I'm.........FLYING!!!" This was no dream, sleepily imagined in a cold, dark hangar. It was *true!* She really *was* flying! No-one could hear her excitement over the roar of her huge engines. All she could see ahead was the deepest blue, cloudless sky. She was climbing – Soaring – FLYING! FiveFiveEight didn't notice the ground disappearing beneath her, with hundreds of cheering people shrinking to tiny specks below, and in no time at all she was at 1,000 feet as The Pilot gently pushed forward on the stick. He was surprised how rapidly she was climbing and, while he'd carefully calculated all her weights and power settings, as he always did before any flight, the one thing he could *never* have anticipated was FiveFiveEight's sheer excitement!

After a few calming words, The Pilot began to explain the importance of the flight to her. He understood why she was so excited (he was too!), but this was the first time that FiveFiveEight had left the ground in over fifteen years, and some important work had to be done to ensure all her equipment was working properly.

Aeroplanes are incredibly complicated, with hundreds of components and systems that need to function perfectly. Only certain things can be tested properly on the ground, but others must be checked whilst flying. Most aeroplanes find Test Flights really boring – nothing exciting *ever* happens, and they typically end up landing exactly where they took off from! Even so, there isn't an aeroplane alive that doesn't understand just how important Test Flying is – if they didn't have to do such dull flights, they wouldn't be allowed to fly at all!

FiveFiveEight certainly wasn't feeling bored! She really didn't care where she was going to land. All she knew was that she was actually *flying*, something which fifteen years before she thought she'd never, ever do again! There are no words to express FiveFiveEight's thoughts as she soared merrily through that crisp autumn sky.

"Right then! Let's see what you can do," said The Pilot, "a few gentle tests just to see all is well." FiveFiveEight's landing gear was still extended, so she knew she would have to keep her speed down for the moment – she really didn't want to damage anything! After a turn to the left, FiveFiveEight settled down into level flight. With more garbled conversation among the Aircrew, it was time to check her undercarriage – it had been tested several times in the hangar while she was still on jacks, but she knew more than anyone just how different things can be whilst airborne.

With all Aircrew eyes on her warning lights, The Pilot moved the undercarriage lever to the "UP" position. FiveFiveEight knew what was expected of her, and she immediately began to fold her long legs up into their bays. She could feel the power of the air rushing past as the first, then the second main leg disappeared snugly into her wings – *Perfect!* With a reassuring "Clunk!", her nose leg folded away neatly, too, and she shut her undercarriage doors, feeling very pleased with herself!

For the first time in years, the smooth, sleek shape of a Vulcan powered majestically through the sky whilst, unbeknown to FiveFiveEight, thousands of people were gazing up at her, shouting and cheering, as she performed flawlessly. The Pilot was impressed, too, but there were still more tests that needed doing before he could truly relax.

After a quick check of his instruments, The Pilot once more pulled back on the stick. Time to climb higher! This time he was ready for FiveFiveEight's sprightly, eager performance, and immediately she responded, raising her nose. Her massive wings sliced through the air, and she steadily reached 2,000 feet – then 3,000 – climbing ever skyward. Her smile grew and grew – *this* is what she was meant to do........... 4,000...........5,000. Test Flights had *never* been this much fun! At 6,000 feet, as requested, she levelled-off, ready for her next test.

Pilots and aeroplanes never have to actually *speak* to one another – they have a language all their own. With even the tiniest movement of hand or foot, an aeroplane knows exactly what they're expected to reply. If an aeroplane isn't feeling well, a Pilot knows instantly and won't ask for too much. When all is well, a Pilot has absolute trust and confidence that the aeroplane will do exactly as requested. There are even some snooty aeroplanes who don't like responding to Pilots at all! As you might imagine, few Pilots like flying *them!*

Vulcans have *never* been snooty, though, and FiveFiveEight was keen to show The Pilot how fantastic she was feeling. Now that she was straight and level once again, The Pilot moved the stick, first to one side then the other – only very slightly, as Vulcans are extremely agile and precise. FiveFiveEight knew exactly what he wanted from her – gentle turns, first to the left then to the right, just to see if there were any handling problems. She was more than capable of pulling incredibly tight turns when required, but now was *not* the time for that! She wanted to show The Pilot just how fit, healthy and well balanced she was. Anyway, she didn't need to show off – not *yet*, anyway! FiveFiveEight's perfect manoeuvres told The Pilot everything he wanted to know. All was fine and working perfectly.

After a few more general flying checks, some at high speed some slower, The Pilot was hugely impressed with FiveFiveEight's performance and decided it was time to head for home. The Aircrew had enjoyed it just as much as FiveFiveEight – after all, *they* hadn't flown her for fifteen years, *either!* They'd only been airborne for thirty minutes, but it was the most exhilarating thirty minutes of FiveFiveEight's entire life!

All too soon, FiveFiveEight spotted the airfield in front of her. She really didn't want to land – she was having too much fun! But The Pilot lowered her undercarriage anyway, and all FiveFiveEight's legs locked firmly into place as she slowed. She didn't need to land immediately, though, and easily had enough fuel for a flypast over the heads of the countless multi-coloured human specks still cheering below! In all her years of wowing crowds, there had never been an occasion quite like this, and she wanted to make the most of it!

In no time at all she was ready to land. *This* was going to be tricky – after all, she hadn't landed *anywhere* for fifteen years, and she really couldn't afford to mess it up with so many people watching! She extended her airbrakes – approaching too fast would make landing very difficult, too slowly and she might not even reach the runway! She was *very* nervous, but The Pilot had every confidence in her and, with expert inputs to her stick and rudder, she was perfectly lined up with the runway and at the perfect speed – 135 knots. Now it was all up to her, and she couldn't remember a time when a runway had looked so *tiny!*

With all the concentration she could muster, FiveFiveEight watched as the tarmac rose toward her, getting bigger and bigger the closer she got. At just the perfect moment, she reached out with her main undercarriage legs and, with the tiniest squeak of her tyres, she was down! Little puffs of smoke briefly spiralled up behind as she confidently rested her weight firmly on the ground. There was no time to relax, however, she was moving very fast and still had to stop!

The Pilot kept her absolutely straight on the centre-line as, with gritted teeth, she applied her brakes. She kept her nose as high as possible, which would help to slow her down and stop her brakes getting too hot. Before she knew it, she had slowed to a walking pace – despite her nerves, it was one of the best landings she'd ever made!

After taxiing back to the hangar, the Aircrew went through another lengthy checklist as they shut down all FiveFiveEight's systems, then climbed out to a deafening cheer from all the fans and supporters jostling around her.

In all the commotion, The Pilot stopped, turned, and looked up at FiveFiveEight with a slight smile on his face. No words were needed. They each knew what the other was thinking.

She'd Done It! After all those years, FiveFiveEight was a *real* aeroplane again!

Aircraft Type:	Handley Page Victor B2
Age:	40 Something!
Born:	4th May 1963 - Radlett UK
Height:	30 feet 1 Inch
Length:	114 feet 11 Inches
Wingspan:	120 feet
Weight:	233,000 lb
Colour-scheme:	Hemp
Previous Job:	V Bomber and Tanker
Current Job:	Retired and Resting
Hobbies:	Taxiing, Being Naughty, Making Noise, Blowing Up Clouds of Dust!
Dislikes:	Vulcans (only Joking ☺) Cheeky Fighter Aircraft Rain

M.D.

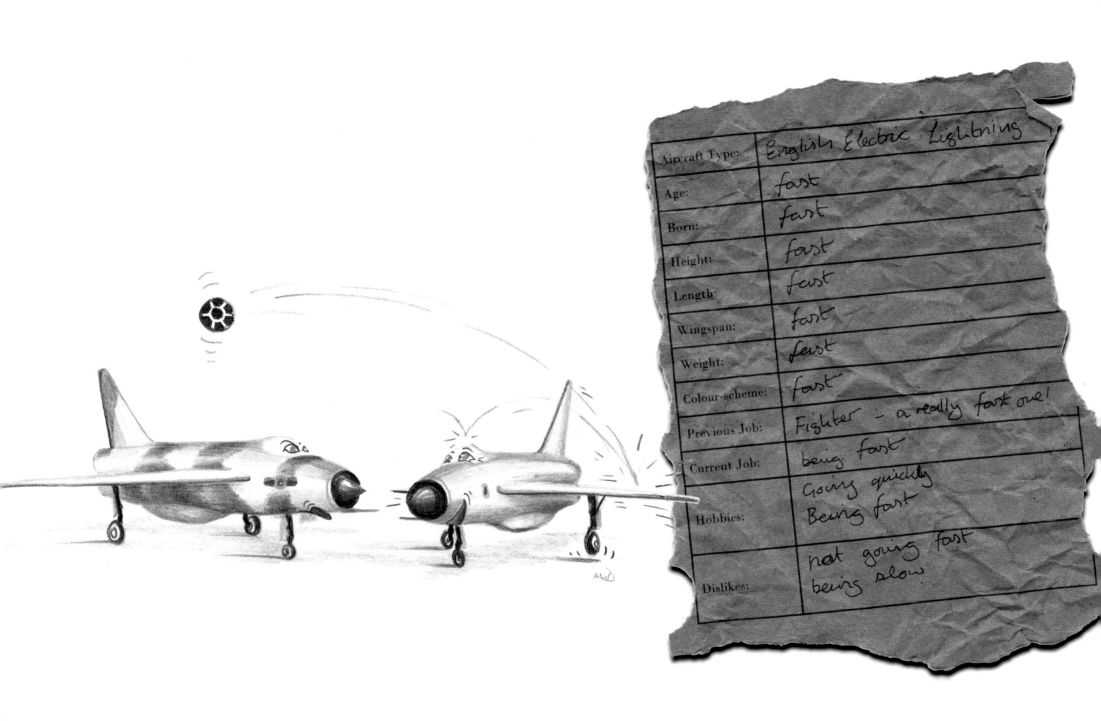

Aircraft Type:	AVRO VULCAN B2
Age:	▓▓ Shhh!!!
Born:	1st JULY 1960 - WOODFORD, UK
Height:	21ft 1in
Length:	99ft 11in
Wingspan:	111ft
Weight:	~~POUNDS~~ NOT TELLING!!
Colour-scheme:	~~WHITE~~ GREY & GREEN
Previous Job:	BOMBER / TANKER
Current Job:	MAKING CHILDREN SAY "WOW!"
Hobbies:	TAKING OFF (NOISILY!!) SETTING OFF CAR ALARMS! FLYING THROUGH FLUFFY WHITE CLOUDS WING - WAVING
Dislikes:	BORING HANGARS THUNDERSTORMS BLACK CLOUDS VERY SHORT RUNWAYS!

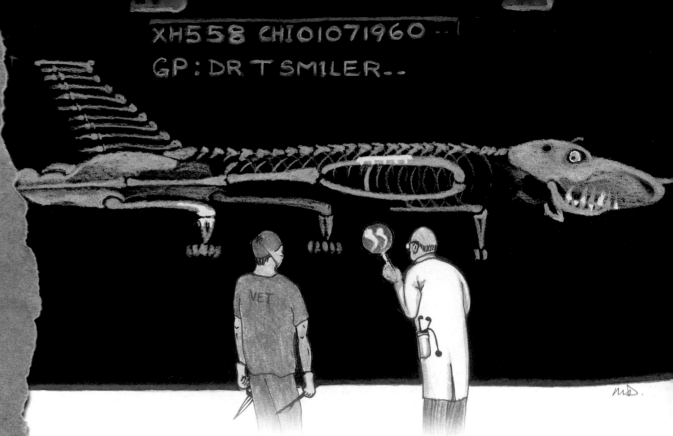

XH558 CHI0I071960..

GP: DR T SMILER..

How many autographs from FiveFiveEight's crew can you collect?

Why not get to know FiveFiveEight yourself?

Ask your Mum and Dad about joining our Club today - you can even join as a family!

Call: 0116 247 8145

Or join online at www.VulcantotheSky.org